MW01598171

Halloween Pizza Murder

Papa Pacelli's Pizzeria Series

Book Eighteen

By

Patti Benning

<u>Author's Note:</u> On the next page, you'll find out how to access all of my books easily, as well as locate books by best-selling author, Summer Prescott. I'd love to hear your thoughts on my books, the storylines, and anything else that you'd like to comment on – reader feedback is very important to me. Please see the following page for my publisher's contact information. If you'd like to be on her list of "folks to contact" with updates, release and sales notifications, etc...just shoot her an email and let her know. Thanks for reading!

Also...

...if you're looking for more great reads, from me and Summer, check out the Summer Prescott Publishing Book Catalog:

http://summerprescottbooks.com/book-catalog/ for some truly delicious stories.

Contact Info for Summer Prescott Publishing:

Twitter: @summerprescott1

Blog and Book Catalog: http://summerprescottbooks.com

Email: summer.prescott.cozies@gmail.com

And…look up The Summer Prescott Fan Page and Summer Prescott Publishing Page on Facebook – let's be friends!

To sign up for our fun and exciting newsletter, which will give you opportunities to win prizes and swag, enter contests, and be the first to know about New Releases, click here:

https://forms.aweber.com/form/02/1682036602.htm

TABLE OF CONTENTS

HALLOWEEN PIZZA
MURDER

Papa Pacelli's Pizzeria Series Book Eighteen

CHAPTER ONE

Eleanora Pacelli pulled on her jacket and slid her purse's strap over her shoulder. She bent down to say a quick goodbye to her dog, then walked out the front door, locking it behind her. It was the beginning of her first full day back from Florida, and she was in a good mood. It had been wonderful to sleep in her own bed for the first night in a week, and it had been even better to have Bunny, her black and white papillon, sleep on the pillow beside her head.

She had to admit, it was disconcerting to know that Nonna would no longer be waiting at home for her when she got done with work. She was truly alone now, and she wasn't sure what she would do with the big, empty house all to herself.

Earlier that morning, she had spoken to her grandmother, who was as happy as a clam in the retirement community down in Florida. She was glad to be able to regain some of her independence, and was looking forward to a snow-free winter. Ellie was planning to visit her again around Christmastime, and was eager to see how Nonna had transformed the modest little condo into a home.

Outside, she was greeted by the crisp, autumn air. She inhaled deeply, glad to be back in Maine. It was a beautiful fall day, with only a few fluffy white clouds in the sky, and a breeze that made the dry leaves scuttle across the ground. Halloween was quickly approaching, as her nearest neighbor's yard attested. Her own yard was bare; she had been so distracted by the trip to Florida that she hadn't even paused to think of the coming holiday.

Tomorrow, she would have to go down into the basement and bring up some of her grandmother's boxes of decorations. She loved decorating for the holidays, and she didn't want to miss out on Halloween this year, even though she was a bit late to the game.

She got into the driver's seat of her car, letting the engine warm-up for a couple of minutes before she went anywhere. She shot one last look at the house, realizing that Bunny and Marlowe, her grandfather's greenwing macaw, would both be alone until she got home that evening. They were used to having Nonna there to take care of them and keep them company, but now they were going to have to be alone every day while she worked. She hoped they would adjust to the new routine quickly. If she had time, maybe she would start to come home during her breaks to check on them.

Ellie felt her heart lift as she pulled into the Papa Pacelli's lot. Even though the pizzeria in Florida had been renovated to look like the original restaurant, there was still something special about the pizzeria that her grandfather had opened over twenty years ago. It would always hold its own place in her heart.

She was glad to see that her employees had already decorated the restaurant for the holiday. She had mentioned it to Pete before she left, but she hadn't been sure if he would remember. The table centerpieces had been replaced with little ceramic jack-o'-lanterns, and bats had been hung from the ceiling. Fake spider webs clung to the corners of the counter, and a banner that read *Have a Happy Halloween!* had been hung just under the menu.

She smiled, feeling a rush of pride at how well her employees had done in her absence. She knew that she had been right to trust them with the pizzeria while she was gone. In fact, they had done so well that she thought she would feel comfortable taking even more trips in the future. She wanted to be an active part of the Florida pizzeria, which meant flying down there at least a couple of times a year so she could be hands-on for a couple of days.

The next few hours were some of the most relaxing ones she had ever had at work. It was nice to be in a familiar kitchen, serving her regular customers, knowing that her fiancé was only a few blocks away at the sheriff's department. She had a lot to catch up on now that she was back, including seeing her best friend Shannon and thanking her for watching the animals. She couldn't wait to tell her friend about the beautiful wedding dress she had picked out in Florida. It was the first major step she taken in planning her wedding, and it made her look forward to the big day even more.

She had a list of other tasks she wanted to complete this week, which included renting a venue for the wedding. She and Russell still needed to set a date, but she was thinking it would be sometime early next year. She wanted a late winter wedding, so that she and Russell would have time for a honeymoon before her grandmother returned.

At four, her newest employee, Pete, joined her for his shift. He had been the only one not to join them on their trip to Florida. Ellie felt a bit bad about that; he hadn't been working there very long, and he didn't seem as much a part of their team as the others did, but that would resolve itself in time. He was good-natured and responsible, and she was glad that she had decided to hire him.

However, they were still an employee short. A few weeks ago, one of their employees had been killed on the job, and it had devastated the entire crew. She would feel terrible replacing her, but it couldn't be helped. It wasn't fair to ask her employees to work so much, and with the holidays coming up, she needed someone who could take the pressure off of all of them.

13

It was just one more thing to add to her to-do list for this week. She knew that she would spend the next few days playing catch-up. She had missed a lot while she was gone though she wouldn't have traded the trip for anything. It was worth it to be there for the opening of the second pizzeria.

"Hi, Ms. P.," Pete said when he got in. "How is it going?"

"It was hectic, but the restaurant is doing well. How were things here?"

She had left Florida on a good note, although they had run into several problems while she was there. The three employees were off to a great start. She had high hopes for the success of the restaurant, even though she knew it would be at least a couple of months before they began to break even with all of the money she had poured into the place. Hopefully by this time next year, the profits would have started to come in. She wasn't sure whether she would open other restaurants in the future. While it was satisfying to see the Papa Pacelli sign in another state, and it was gratifying to know that she had successfully opened a second restaurant on her own, it had been a lot of work, and it had been very stressful. She had spent months planning and preparing. If she decided to go ahead and open a third restaurant, it would be a couple of years down the line.

"Everything has been going fine," he said. "People are excited for Halloween. Oh, I've been meaning to ask you, do you have anything planned for the restaurant?"

"I don't have any big plans this year," Ellie told him. "I've been too busy. We'll just hand out candy the day of."

"Do you mind if we wear costumes to work?"

"Not at all, as long as they don't interfere with your work. Just make sure it's safe for the kitchen."

"Okay," he said, grinning. "I'll have to come up with something fun."

She would have to find a Halloween costume too, she realized. She couldn't be the only one in the restaurant without one. *I wonder if Russell wants to do anything that evening?* He would probably be working. Halloween was one of the busier nights for the police, and Russell was never one to shirk his job. Maybe she could tag along after the pizzeria closed for the evening. She enjoyed riding along with him, and getting a glimpse into his life. It would definitely beat sitting at home alone, which was her other option now that her grandmother was living in Florida. Besides, spending time with him was always the highlight of her week.

CHAPTER TWO

It had been an easy day, and she was still full of energy when she got home that evening. After taking care of the animals, who had both been thrilled to see her after being alone all day, she went down into the basement to fetch the box of Halloween decorations that she had stored down there the year before.

Her grandmother's basement was dark and crowded. There were decades worth of boxes, old furniture, and plenty of clutter everywhere. Some of the light bulbs had burned out, and she had no way to reach them without climbing over a sea of junk. Then, of course, there were the cobwebs, which seemed to multiply every time she went down there. She didn't like the basement at all, and she had big plans to clean it out at some point, but never seemed to get around to it. Now, it would have to wait until her grandmother's return in the spring. She didn't want to take the liberty of tossing her grandparents' possessions without Nonna there to tell her what to keep.

Thankfully, the Halloween box was close to the stairway, since she had used it only the year before. She lugged it up the stairs and set it down in the living room. With Bunny following doggedly at her heels, she began removing the decorations and placing them around the house. Remembering how frightened Marlowe had been of the hanging decorations last year, she refrained from putting any near the bird cage. She wouldn't bother putting spider webs inside, either; they were just too messy to be worth the hassle and she hated running into them unexpectedly in the dark.

Once she had finished with her favorite indoor decorations, she went back to the basement and found a couple of things to go outside, including an old, creepy scarecrow. She put it in the middle of the yard, and found an old black sheet in the basement, pulling it up in a hood around the scarecrow's head to make it look like the Grim Reaper. She stepped back, smiling at the effect. Her yard wasn't the only bare one on the street anymore.

Not that it mattered much. They never had very many trick-or-treaters this far out of town. She would just leave a bowl of candy on the front porch for the few people that ventured out this way. The pizzeria was another story; she knew it would be busy the night of the holiday, and they would have to stock up on candy in advance. She was looking forward to seeing all of the costumes, though she still had to find something to wear herself.

She realized with a start that this was it. She had nothing left to do that evening. The house was clean, all of her bills were paid, and she had no other commitments. Without Nonna there, she had absolutely nothing to do until she went to work the next day. It was an odd feeling, and not completely good. Was this going to be her life from now on? She rarely got to the pizzeria before eleven, and usually didn't work weekends. She was used to driving her grandmother to appointments a couple of times a week, and spending a lot of time talking daily with the older woman. With so much free time suddenly on her hands, maybe she could get into a hobby. But what?

Suddenly she remembered an idea that she had played around with a couple of months ago, which she had temporarily forgotten while she worked through all of the issues with the second pizzeria. The small business club. There were a lot of small business owners in town, and it would be nice to get to know them all better. It would give her something to focus on besides work. While she loved her job, she needed more in her life.

Where could we meet? she wondered. The answer was obvious; since she no longer had to worry about disturbing her grandmother, the small business club could meet in the Pacelli house. It would be nice to have people over once or twice a month and talk about all of the goings on at each of their businesses. If they got organized, maybe they could even start planning a couple of events each year.

Feeling better now that she had decided to do something, she went back inside, shutting the door firmly behind her and turning the deadbolt. She still wasn't completely comfortable living alone outside of town; the last time she had lived alone, she had been in an apartment surrounded by everyone else in her building. If she needed help, she could have gone to anyone else on her floor.

Still, it was nice to have her own home again. It was pleasantly warm inside, and smelled like the lasagna that was currently cooking in the kitchen. It should be just about ready to come out, then she would have just enough time for a nice dinner and half an hour of reading before she went to bed.

"Sorry you were alone for so long today," she said to Marlowe, walking up to the bird's cage on her way to the kitchen. "We'll try to figure out a new schedule. Things are going to have to change without Nonna here, but we'll make do, won't we?" She scratched the bird between the bars of the cage, then continued on to the kitchen to take the lasagna out of the oven.

She grabbed the oven mitts and pulled open the oven door. The cheesy top of the lasagna was the perfect golden-brown color that she liked. She pulled it just as Bunny started yapping behind her.

"What are you doing?" Ellie asked, turning to face the little dog, who was standing in front of the glass kitchen door.

Standing on the other side of the door was a woman, dressed all in white. Ellie screamed and the lasagna slipped out of her hands, splattering on the floor. She hardly registered the hot pasta sauce that stung her toes. Her eyes were glued on the woman at the door.

The woman's dark hair was loose and windblown, partially covering her face. She was standing just inches from the glass, staring straight at Ellie. Ellie couldn't look away, her heart hammering in her chest. Bunny was still barking, dancing fearlessly in front of the door. The woman raised one hand, reaching towards the glass. There was something dark staining the sleeves of her white dress. Was it blood?

Knowing that something was deeply wrong, she backpedaled, only turning when she felt the counter behind her. She reached for the knife block and pulled out the biggest one she had, before turning back around. The woman was gone.

Shaken, Ellie approached the door cautiously. Bunny had fallen silent, but was still staring intently into the darkness outside. She reached over and clicked on the patio light. There was nothing there. She took a deep breath. It had probably just been a Halloween prank. Some people took the holiday little bit too seriously. Still, she made

21

sure that the door was locked, then went to the front door and double checked that one as well. She was glad that her bedroom was on the second floor. She probably wouldn't get much sleep that night.

She glanced at her phone, considering whether to call Russell. He wouldn't be able to do anything; it would just worry him. And if he came over to check on her, it would add hours to her evening. She was already tired. It was something that she could mention to him in the morning. For now, she had to clean up the lasagna, find something else for dinner, then go to bed. If she noticed anything else unusual during the night, she would call him then. She slipped her cell phone into her pocket, just in case.

CHAPTER THREE

The next morning dawned grey and misty. Ellie woke up early, still unsettled by what she had seen the night before. It seemed a lot less frightening in the morning's light, however, and she found herself thinking more about the wrecked lasagna than the creepy woman.

Since she had plenty of time on her hands before she went to work, she decided to make herself a nice big breakfast, just like her grandmother used to. She dug around in the pantry, gathering all of the ingredients, then got to work on chocolate chip muffins. It may not be the healthiest breakfast in the world, but Ellie decided that she could use some comfort food.

She followed the recipe she had found online, adding the semi-sweet chocolate chips last. She tasted a dollop of the batter and smiled. Perfect. She poured the mix into the muffin pan and put it in the oven, washing the dishes before returning upstairs to get dressed for the day. When she came back downstairs, she would get started on the bacon and eggs.

As she was pulling on her sweater, she heard her cell phone ring downstairs. After a few seconds, the ringer stopped as the phone went to voicemail, then started back up again immediately. Ellie hurried to finish getting dressed and went downstairs, beginning to worry as the phone rang a third time. Who could want to talk to her so urgently? Had something happened to her grandmother?

Just as she reached the kitchen, the phone began to ring once more. The caller ID told her it was Russell. She answered.

"Thank goodness," he said.

"Russell?" she said. "What's going on? What's wrong?"

"I just got a call about a body found in the state park near your house. The description was of a middle-aged woman with dark hair. I was so worried that –"

He broke off, his voice rough. She understood.

"I'm fine," she said. His description of the victim struck her like a punch. A woman with dark hair, found in the woods near her house. "Oh, Russell," she said. "I think I saw her last night."

25

"What do you mean?" he asked.

She told him about the woman dressed in white that she had seen at the back door. "I thought it was someone pulling a Halloween prank," she said. "I should have said something. She just vanished. I had no idea that she needed help."

"Can you come down to the sheriff's department before work and make an official police report?" he asked.

"Of course," she said. "I can be there in about an hour. I just put muffins in the oven, but I'll leave as soon as they're done."

"Okay," he said. "Thank you, Ellie. I'm going to go look at the body. I'll meet you at the sheriff's department in an hour. I'm sorry if I worried you, it's just... well, I'm sure you can imagine."

She could. If their positions had been switched and she had heard about a body matching his description, she would have been frantic. She regretted not telling him about the woman sooner. The heavy weight of guilt settled on her chest. Had her actions caused someone's death?

After putting the muffins on the counter to cool, she finished getting ready to go. When she was about to leave, she dumped the muffins

26

into a big plastic container and put a lid on it, planning to take them down to the sheriff's department to share. She said a quick goodbye to the animals and left.

Mrs. Lafferre greeted her at the front desk. She left the older woman two of the chocolate chip muffins before going into the back to meet Russell in his office. He was pale and tired, but smiled at her when she came in.

"Hey, I'm glad you're here," he said. "You said you saw the woman last night?"

"Yes," Ellie said, taking one of the seats across from him and putting the container of muffins on the desk. "It was around ten or ten-thirty."

He shook his head, but he was smiling. She frowned, confused. "It couldn't have been her," he said. "Early estimates place her time of death at least forty-eight hours ago. There's no way that you saw her just twelve hours ago."

Ellie blinked. She was relieved, but it didn't explain what she had seen. Maybe she had been right the first time and it had just been a Halloween prank.

27

"Do you know who she was?" Ellie asked.

"No," Russell said. "She was found without anything on her. No wallet, no ID, not even a medical alert bracelet to help us identify her. She was only wearing a white dress. Here, I have a photo of her taken at the crime scene. Maybe you'll recognize her – you see a lot of people coming through the pizzeria."

He pulled open a file and took out a printed picture, which he slid across the desk to her. Ellie stared at it, feeling her fingers go cold. This *was* the woman she had seen the night before. She recognized the long dark hair and the white dress.

"Russell…" She trailed off, not sure how to explain it. What had she seen? How was this possible?

"What is it?" he asked, frowning and leaning forward in concern.

"This is the woman I saw," she said. "I don't know how, or if it's even possible, but I did. I saw her. I saw her last night, standing on my back porch, looking right at me."

"Ellie, I told you, there's no way that this woman has been dead for only twelve hours."

28

"I know what I saw," she said. "Look, she was at my back door last night. I'm not making this up. Bunny saw her and started barking. I turned away for a second and when I turned back, she was gone. It was late enough that I didn't want to call and disturb you, but now I'm thinking that I should have. You don't believe me, do you?"

"I do," he said, his brows drawn together. "At least, I believe that *you* believe you saw something. It couldn't have been the victim, though. This woman wasn't alive at ten-thirty last night. Are you sure you didn't have a bad dream, and then you just connected the dots in the morning when I called you?"

"I wasn't dreaming," she said, beginning to get annoyed. "When I saw her, I dropped a lasagna all over the floor. I certainly didn't dream cleaning it up. It's still in my garbage bin."

"I'm sorry," he said. "I'm not saying you're wrong. I just don't know how to explain this."

Ellie nodded. "Trust me, I have no idea what to think about any of this either. Do you know how she died?"

"She had a stab wound. The knife entered between her ribs and nicked her heart. The poor woman managed to get away from her assailant, but only made it a couple hundred yards into the woods before she collapsed."

29

"I know you said she was found near my house. How close was she?"

"You know the trails that go through the state park into the forest behind the Pacelli house?" She nodded. "She was found along those, almost directly back from your house, about a quarter of a mile in. A dog walker found her while he was out for a morning jog with his lab before work. He called it in at about eight this morning."

Ellie bit her lip. It couldn't be a coincidence, not with the body found so close to her house. She wasn't crazy. She knew who she had seen, the only question was how.

CHAPTER FOUR

Ellie was horribly distracted during work that day, making mistakes that she hadn't made since she had first started working at the pizzeria. She burnt one of the first orders, which threw her whole schedule off, making the next couple of orders late. By the time Rose got there, she was a wreck.

"Ms. P., what's wrong?" her employee asked, fanning away smoke from the splatters of pizza sauce Ellie had spilled on one of the burners.

"I'm sorry," Ellie said. "I know it's a mess in here. Today's been terrible."

"Did something happen to your grandmother or one of the animals?"

"No, no, nothing like that. There's been a murder, and it was near my house. It has me pretty shaken up."

31

"Oh no, was it anyone you knew? That's horrible."

"No, I didn't know her," Ellie said. She didn't want to get into the more complicated matter of what had happened the night before. Not yet, anyway. Not until she knew for sure what had happened. "It happened only a quarter mile away from my house, though."

"Are you going to be okay out there on your own?" Rose asked, her eyes wide with concern. "Do they know who did it?"

"They don't have any leads yet," she replied. "I'm sure I'll be fine." The truth was, she hadn't even thought about that at all. Would she be safe all the way out there, alone, so close to the site of a murder? She bit her lip. It was one more thing to worry about.

"No offense, Ms. P., but you look terrible. Do you want to go home? I know Iris wouldn't mind the extra hours, and I'm sure she'd be happy to come in. She wants to buy a new car, so she's trying to work as much as possible."

It was tempting. Ellie had already made a mess of things there, and she didn't see her mood improving for the rest of the day.

"If she doesn't mind coming in on such short notice, I'll switch shifts with her," Ellie said. "I'll give her a call. Thanks, Rose. I feel bad about leaving early, but I'm obviously not going to be much help here today."

"I'm going to go clock in, then I'll help clean up the mess back here. Be careful when you get home. I can't imagine how frightening it must be for you."

It felt good to get out of the restaurant, even though it was still a dreary day. Now that Rose had mentioned it, she couldn't stop thinking about the fact that there was a killer out there somewhere, and he had committed a murder not far from her home. Earlier in the day, she had been too distracted by thoughts of the woman that she had seen to think about that, but now she couldn't get it out of her head. Even though she wasn't at work, she didn't want to go home. Not now, not alone. She decided to call Shannon and see if her friend wanted to meet somewhere to talk.

"I'm actually heading to an interview right now," her friend said when she answered the call. "You can tag along, if you want. I think you know the guy – it's Steve, the hotdog shop owner's husband? He bought the little coffee shop that closed down, as I'm sure you know, and I was going to do a small piece in the newspaper about his plans for the building. We're just meeting for lunch at the hotdog shop."

"Perfect, I'll meet you there soon," Ellie said. "Thanks, I really need this. Something happened; I'll tell you about it later."

She pulled into Hot Diggity Dog's parking lot a few minutes later. Shannon's vehicle was already there, along with a smattering of other cars. She was glad to see that the place was doing well. Joanna, the restaurant owner, was a likable woman, and she deserved the success. Ellie had helped her open the restaurant a couple of months ago, and the two of them had stayed in touch. Now that she was done working so hard on the second pizzeria, she would have more time to explore their new friendship. She remembered her idea for the small business club, and decided to ask Joanna about it today. She could be the very first member.

Inside, she saw Shannon already sitting at a table with food in front of her. Steve was nowhere to be seen, so Ellie walked over to join her.

"Hey," her friend said, rising to give her a hug. "It's good to see you. I'm glad you're back. We have a lot to catch up on. You said you had something you wanted to tell me?"

"We can talk about that later," Ellie said. She didn't want to discuss the murder in such a public place. "Where's Steve?"

"He's running a few minutes behind," Shannon said. "I'm just grabbing lunch while I wait. Go ahead and order something and join me."

Deciding that one of Joanna's top-of-the-line hotdogs sounded good, she walked up to the counter and saw a familiar face. "Hi, Clara," she said, smiling at her old employee. "How is it going here?"

"Great," Clara said. "How did the Florida trip go?"

"The restaurant is doing well," Ellie said. "It's too bad you couldn't come. I think the other employees really enjoyed the getaway."

"I'm sure was fun," the other woman said. "I miss everyone at the pizzeria, but I love working here. What can I get you?"

"Let's see…" Ellie gazed at the menu for a moment. "I'll have a hot dog on a wheat bun, topped with sauerkraut, dill pickles, and onions. I'll also take a soda to drink."

"Coming right out," Clara said. "I'll tell Joanna you're here, I'm sure she'll want to come say hi."

A couple of minutes later, the restaurant's owner came out to bring Ellie her order herself. Joanna took the seat across from her and Shannon.

"I'm glad you stopped in," she said. "It's been a while, hasn't it?"

"It has," Ellie agreed. "I've been so busy with the restaurant in Florida, I haven't really had time for much else. I want to start getting more involved now, though. Speaking of that, how would you feel about joining a small business club that I would be hosting? We could meet one or two times a month. We can discuss things relevant to running our businesses, and also just take the time to get to know one another."

"I think that sounds wonderful," Joanna said. "You mentioned something about that a while back, didn't you? Do you know anyone else who would be joining?"

"Not yet," Ellie said. "I only just decided to go through with it. You're the first person I asked."

"Well, I'm honored," her friend said. "And Shannon, I'm sorry Steve's late. He hasn't been himself lately. I think he just has too many projects going on at once."

"It's fine," Shannon said. "I don't mind. I don't have much else I have to do today, anyway. It's nice to stop and get lunch with the two of you."

Ellie agreed. It was nice to spend some time with her friends and not worry about anything else. She hoped to have the chance to do this more often now.

The restaurant's front door opened and she looked around to see Steve, Joanna's husband, come in. He walked over and gave his wife a kiss on the cheek before sitting next to her.

"Sorry," he said. "I got held up. Hopefully I'm not too late?"

"Nope, we've got plenty of time," Shannon said. "If you're ready, let's start with –" She broke off as her phone buzzed. "Shoot, it's from work. They want me to go talk to the sheriff after this and see if he can make any comments about the murder."

Both Joanna and Steve had blank looks on their face. Neither of them must have heard about the murder yet.

"Who got killed?" Joanna asked.

"No one knows," Shannon said. "The woman didn't have any form of identification on her. James told me all about it before he left

37

earlier this afternoon for work. Here, the paper has a photo of her that we're printing in tomorrow's headline."

She held her phone out to Joanna, who gasped. "I know this lady. Steve, isn't she your ex?"

He took the phone from his wife and frowned. "That does look a lot like Melanie," he said. "But I don't see how it can be her. She lives in Portland. What would she be doing all the way up here?"

"We need to tell Russell if you think you know her," Shannon said. "Here, give me her full name and any contact information you have. I'll take it to him when I stop by the sheriff's department later."

She wrote down the information, then continued with the interview. Ellie only half listened, too distracted by the unexpected possible connection between her friend's husband and the dead woman. It couldn't be a coincidence, could it? Was Steve involved with her death somehow? His face gave nothing away, but the chilling thought wouldn't leave her.

CHAPTER FIVE

Russell Ward looked at his sister-in-law, unsettled by the news that she had brought him. Steve had already gotten a reputation around town, and it wasn't a good one. Many of the townspeople were old-fashioned, and they didn't like all of the big plans he had for the properties he was buying. Now, it was coming to his attention that the man had a possible connection to the woman who had been found murdered in the woods behind Ellie's house. An ex-girlfriend, someone who might have had dirt on him that she was using to blackmail. It was a possible motive, and one that he couldn't overlook. If this woman was who Steve and his wife said she was, that would make Steve their lead – and only – suspect in the case.

"Thanks for telling me," he said to Shannon. "How did he act when he saw her photo?"

"He looked surprised," his sister-in-law said. "He didn't even seem to know that she was in town. I know what you're thinking, I don't

40

think anyone could be that good of an actor. You might want to ask Ellie, though. She was watching him the entire time I was doing the interview."

"Ellie was there?"

"Yeah, she met me for lunch."

He frowned. How did his fiancé keep getting involved in these situations? She was like a magnet for danger. He was already concerned that the attack had happened so close to her home. Now, it turned out that she had been there when the man who might be their only suspect had been connected to the murder. That would put her on Steve's radar, and that wasn't a good thing.

"What's with the look on your face?" his sister-in-law asked.

"I just don't like how connected Ellie is to this case," he said. "First, she swears that she saw this woman last night, and now she's there when you link Steve to the victim. She lives a quarter of a mile away from where this woman was attacked. I'm worried about her."

"What do you mean, she saw the woman last night? James told me that she had already been dead for forty-eight hours when you found her."

41

He mentally kicked herself for mentioning his fiancée's experience the night before. She must have had a reason to not tell Shannon. He shouldn't have brought it up.

"We're still trying to figure out what's going on," he said. "If you get a chance to talk to her again, see how she's doing. I hope she knows to call me if she needs anything."

"I'm sure she will," Shannon said. "We didn't get much of a chance to talk about what happened. We had lunch with Steve and Joanna, then I left to come straight here. I'm supposed to be getting a statement from you about the murder for the paper."

He chuckled. "They always send you when they want something from me, don't they? I suppose they think you'll have a better chance than someone else would at getting information out of me."

"It works, doesn't it? You can't say no to your sister-in-law, especially not when she's pregnant."

"Well, it won't work this time. There just isn't much that we know. We're keeping some things quiet, of course. I can tell you that she was found in the state park after what appears to be a violent attack. She had already been dead for some time when she was found. Her identity has yet to be confirmed, and right now we're treating the case as a homicide."

He watched as she scribbled in her notebook. "Is that all? Any idea what the murder weapon was?"

"We have some idea, but it's one of the things I want to keep away from the general public while the investigation is ongoing. And Shannon, please don't mention the link between her and Steve. I don't want to cause any more trouble than is necessary."

"Understood," she said. "Thanks for seeing me. I need to be getting back home so I can type all of this up and send it in."

"Have a good day," he said. "I'll see you and James later. Don't work too hard. Take care of yourself."

"I will," she promised with a smile. "See you later."

Russell watched her go, feeling tired. The weeks leading up to Halloween were busy enough without a murder to solve. He wished he knew what was going on. Ellie's involvement concerned him deeply, but what could he do about it? They simply didn't have the manpower for him to have someone watch her house every night. She was adamant that she had seen the woman on her patio, and even though he knew it was impossible, the thought chilled him. He knew that she would never make something like that up, but dead people generally didn't walk around.

He decided that he had had enough of sitting in his office for the day. It was time to go out and do some real investigating.

He started where the body had been found. The state park's trails were long and twisting, and it was easy to get lost there without a map. He wondered, not for the first time, what the victim had been doing out there in a white dress. It wasn't the sort of thing most people would wear for a hike through the forest.

He had tasked Liam with confirming her identity, and if his deputy confirmed that she was indeed Melanie Boardman, they would at least be on the first step to solving her death.

As he neared the area in which her body had been found, he slowed down, scanning the forest floor for anything that might possibly be evidence. His deputies had already combed through the forest that morning, but there was always the chance that they might have missed something. He was well aware that he was close to Ellie's house, and remembering what she had said about seeing the woman in white the night before, he began heading that way.

The path that he was following curved in a different direction, and he was faced with the decision of whether to follow it, or head straight through to the forest. He almost turned back, but then he saw a scrap of white caught on a branch a little way ahead. He pushed through the underbrush and grabbed it off of the tree. He couldn't tell for sure if it was the same fabric as the victim's dress, but he thought it might be. He tucked it into a baggie and put it in his pocket. He had his first piece of evidence.

He continued walking through the trees, moving more slowly now and keeping his eyes peeled for any other shreds of fabric that might have been left behind. *What was this doing all the way out here?* he wondered. They had determined that the victim had come from the opposite direction. So why was a shred of her clothing hanging off of one of the trees heading toward Ellie's house?

The forest seemed to clear ahead, and he realized that he was approaching the edge and nearing Ellie's backyard. He hadn't found anything else, and was beginning to wonder if the piece of fabric had been a fluke. It could have been anything, really. Sadly, littering was a problem in the park. People brought plenty of trash in, but didn't take it back out with them.

He reached the edge of the forest and was about to turn around and head back when something in the dirt just before the grass lawn began caught his eye. It was the back half of a footprint, where the person's heel had made an indent in the dirt.

45

He took his cell phone out of his pocket and took a photo of it before marking the area with some yellow tape so they would be able to find it more easily later. He felt the hair on the back of his neck rise. Maybe Ellie hadn't been seeing things. Maybe someone really had visited her yard last night.

CHAPTER SIX

After her lunch with Shannon, Ellie went home. Spending time with her friends had made her feel a lot better, and she realized that there was no point in avoiding her house. The windows and doors all had secure locks, and she would be able to tell if someone had been inside. Besides, her animals needed her. She had the day off of work, and she should spend some time with them.

When she got home, Bunny was ecstatic to see her. The little dog jumped up and down, barking excitedly. Ellie took off her jacket and her shoes, then bent down to pet her. The papillon and had been with her through a lot, and she was grateful for the little dog's constant companionship.

"Hey, you," she said, scratching the dog behind the ears. "Do you want to go on a walk later? Give me an hour or two, then we'll go out."

With the dog following her, she went into the other room and opened Marlowe's cage. She let the macaw climb onto her arm, then carried the bird to her grandfather's office, where a large wooden tree stood by the window. The bird stepped onto her perch and climbed across the branches to look out the window. Ellie smiled. It was good to see Marlowe so happy. While Bunny had been happy to spend time with Shannon and Russell while they had been watching her, the bird wasn't as trusting of other people. She had spent most of the time while Ellie was in Florida locked in her cage, for her own safety and the safety of the people that had been caring for her.

"I'll be right back," she said. "I'm going to go get my laptop, and see how things are going at the other pizzeria."

She went upstairs to where her laptop was still packed in her suitcase. The sight of all of her clothes still neatly folded inside reminded her that she still needed to unpack. She would get to it that evening. It would be nice to have the rest of the day to catch up.

She returned downstairs and turned on her computer, going into her email account. Linda had been sending her daily updates since she had left, and she read through them eagerly. The pizzeria was doing well, just as she had hoped. They were already looking into hiring another employee. Ellie had underestimated how busy it would be, which was a good thing, but meant that Linda, Sandra, and Maria all had their work cut out for them.

After emailing her friend back, congratulating her on a job well done, Ellie began to browse for local venues for the wedding. Her original idea had been to use the community center, but she thought that she might as well see what else was out there. There were a couple of places that advertised outdoor locations for weddings, but it wouldn't be warm enough that early in Maine to have an outdoor wedding.

She also didn't want to have to travel too far. She wanted this to be a small affair, with just family and friends. Kittiport was her home, and that was where she wanted to get married. She decided to just check out the community center later. She would have to see how much it would cost to rent it for a day, and what dates they had available next year. When she had a couple of possibilities, she would see what Russell thought. He would have to see when his parents could travel to town the easiest.

She bit her lip, realizing that her wedding meant an invitation for her mom to travel back to Kittiport. She hadn't seen her mother since she had moved away from Chicago, and even when she had lived in the same city as the other woman, they had often gone weeks or months without speaking. She hadn't even mentioned her engagement to her mother yet. She knew that she wouldn't approve of her getting engaged so soon after things had blown up with her last fiancé, and Ellie just hadn't been in the mood to hear about it. However, the time was coming when she would have to break the news.

With a sigh, she shut her computer. She didn't have to deal with that today. Right now, she would fulfill her promise to Bunny and take the little dog on a nice, leisurely walk before heading back into town to see what the availability of the community center was early next year.

Before leaving for their walk, she let Bunny out the back door so that she could go to the bathroom if she had to. She stood on the patio, watching while the dog sniffed the grass. Suddenly, she saw Bunny's ears perk up, and the papillon looked toward the forest. Ellie followed the dog's gaze, but didn't see anything. The dog's tail began to wag, but she didn't bark.

"What is it?" she asked.

The dog ignored her, but resumed sniffing the grass again a moment later. Ellie gazed at the forest, then frowned. She saw something yellow at the edge of her yard and sighed. Some trash had probably blown over there. She would have to pick it up later.

Remembering how viciously the dog had barked at the woman the night before, she figured it couldn't be anything too dangerous. More likely than not, the papillon had simply seen a squirrel.

They went back inside and she clipped the dog's leash onto her collar. She put on her shoes and pulled on her jacket, then they left through the front door. They turned to the left at the end of the driveway, taking their usual route along the coastal road that led away from town. With the forest on one side and the ocean on the other, it was a very scenic walk. The wind picked at her sleeves, but between her jacket and her sweater, she was warm enough to stay comfortable.

It was hard to imagine that on the other side of the country, her grandmother was enjoying the warm, sunny weather of Florida. "I hope she's happy," she said. "I bet you miss her, don't you?"

Bunny was too intent on sniffing alongside the road to even look up at her. Ellie sighed and looked up at the sky. It was still gray, but it was gradually starting to clear. She inhaled deeply, appreciating the autumn scent of dry leaves. Florida might be warm, but nothing beat home.

After twenty minutes, she was about to suggest that they turn around, when Bunny's ears perked up again and she looked towards the trees. Ellie stopped mid-step and followed the dog's gaze. This time the papillon's tail wasn't wagging. In fact, Ellie could hear a low growl coming from the dog's throat.

Ellie reached for her phone in her pocket and wrapped her fingers around it. She didn't know if she would need it, but she wanted it handy just in case.

Suddenly she saw something through the trees. A flash of white. Ellie felt her heart began to pound. She saw movement again. It was definitely a person, moving away from her and deeper into the woods.

She took her cell phone out and took a picture, and by the time she lowered the device, the person was gone.

"I know I'm not hallucinating that," she said to her dog. "And I have a picture to prove it. Now, should we head back?"

If she was braver, she might head into the woods after the person, but she wasn't eager to put herself in danger without a good reason. Besides, it had probably just been a hiker, or someone who had gotten lost on one of the trails. Russell was right. Dead people didn't walk around.

CHAPTER SEVEN

After getting back to the house and drying off her dog's muddy feet, Ellie took a seat in the kitchen and looked at the photo she had taken with her phone. The quality wasn't the best, but what she could see was chilling. The picture showed a grainy image of someone wearing white, hurrying through the woods. Ellie could see a smudge of dark hair, but not much else. It was impossible to tell for sure whether it was the same woman that she had seen before, but she would be willing to bet on it.

She sent a photo in a text message to Russell, then forced herself to take her mind from the subject. Yes, it was disconcerting, but there wasn't anything that she could do about it now. What she *could* do was make arrangements for her wedding, she might as well take advantage of her free time to do so now.

She drove back into town, this time on a mission to go to the community center instead of on her way to work. She had called

55

ahead, and the person that she wanted to see was available. Dan Asado was the man in charge of renting out portions of the community center. Ellie had met him a couple of times before, and was hopeful that he would be able to give her a good deal.

"Hi, Dan," she said when she got out of her car. He was standing in front of the building, waiting for her. "Thanks for meeting me on such short notice."

"No problem," he said. "I'm always happy to do a favor for a friend of the sheriff's."

"That's actually what I'm here about," she said. "I need a venue for our wedding, and this is the first place that popped into my head."

"Congratulations. Russell's a lucky man. How soon are you hoping to get married?"

"I was hoping to look at dates for some time early next year, late winter."

"Well, come on in. We'll take a look at the calendar. Do you know what day of the week you would want it to be on?"

"I'm not sure yet. I figured I would look at some of the dates you have available, and go talk to Russell about them before getting back to you. We will need to figure things out with our families as well, of course."

"Of course. The office is right this way."

Ellie followed him down a hall she had never been down before to a small room in the back corner of the building. "Wow, you have the main rooms nicely decorated," she said. "Is there something planned for Halloween?"

"We are having an indoor trick-or-treating party for some of the younger kids in town," he said. "It's supposed to be pretty cold the night of Halloween, and some of the parents thought that this would be a better alternative for the youngest kids."

"That's a great idea," she said.

"Here's the calendar. Let me see… how early in the year were you thinking?"

"Sometime in the second half of February or first half of March would be perfect," she said. She wanted to spend some time married to Russell before her grandmother returned. It would be nice to have the house to themselves for a few weeks.

57

"Okay. You're in luck. We are pretty open for those weeks. Here's what we have."

"Do you mind if I take a photo of the schedule? I want to show Russell and see what works best for him."

"Be my guest," he said.

"Thanks. I'll get back to you as soon as I know."

After she was done at the community center, she headed straight to the sheriff's department to talk to Russell. It felt good to be finally making some progress towards their wedding. With a dress and soon a location, they would be well on their way to actually getting married.

"It's just me again," she said, knocking at his office door and walking in.

"Is everything okay?" he asked, looking up from his desk. He was wearing a jacket, which he hadn't been wearing before, and his car keys were sitting in front of him along with a spread of files.

"Yes," she said. "I just wanted to have you help me pick out a wedding date. I just stopped by the community center and spoke to Dan, who gave me a few dates in February that might work."

"Go ahead and sit down," he said. "I just got back, sorry everything is a mess. I decided to take a break from sitting in my office and do some field work."

"Did you find anything new pertaining to the case?" she asked. She took the same seat she had had that morning and pried open the container with the muffins, which she had accidentally left there.

"Possibly," he said. He hesitated, and for a moment she thought he was about to continue, but then he said, "So, what are the possible dates?"

She showed him the photos she had taken of the schedule, and they discussed which date they wanted for a few minutes. Eventually, they settled on two different days that they liked. He promised to call his parents and see which one would be better for them.

"I'll have to call my mom, too," she said. "She might want to stay for a couple of days. She did grow up here, after all."

"It will be nice to meet her," Russell said.

"Yeah… I suppose it will be nice to see her again, too. We've never really been the best about communicating with each other, to be honest. I'm a little bit worried about telling her about our engagement."

"You haven't told her yet?" he asked, looking surprised.

"I haven't had a chance," she said. "I've been focused on getting the second pizzeria opened, and I didn't want any distractions."

"I hope it goes well when you tell her," he said. "My parents were happy for us. My mom's really come around since she met you."

Ellie smiled. His mother hadn't been her greatest fan when they had first met, but they had patched things up towards the end of her visit. She was glad to his parents were happy that he was remarrying. She liked his family, and would be proud to be a part of it.

Taking her phone back from him, she remembered the photo that she had snapped earlier. "Oh, there's something else I need to show you," she said.

She found the photo and zoomed in. Handing phone over to him, she said, "While I was walking Bunny earlier today, I saw that woman again. At least, I'm pretty sure it was her. I managed to snap a photo. It's not great, but it shows that someone was there."

60

"When was this?" he asked.

"Maybe around three-thirty?" she said.

"I wish you would have called me," he said. "I would have been in the area around then."

"She was already gone by the time I got done snapping the photo," she replied. "I told you, I saw her. This is proof. Something odd is going on."

"Well, it can't be the woman who died," he said. "I don't have an explanation for this, Ellie. Are you sure this is the same person you saw last night?"

"I'm not," she admitted. "It could have been anyone."

"I'll drive the area again later today," he said. "If you see anyone wandering around again, call me immediately, okay?"

She nodded. "I will," she promised. She was frustrated. No, she couldn't swear that this was the same person she had seen, but it was too much of a coincidence for her to believe it wasn't related. There was a woman in white wandering the woods near her house. Who was she? Had Ellie seen a ghost?

CHAPTER EIGHT

Ellie kept the outdoor lights on all night. With Bunny sleeping on the pillow beside her head, she felt secure. Both times the mysterious woman had been around, the dog had alerted her, and tonight the papillon slept through the night without twitching once.

In the morning, she went through the normal routine of feeding the animals and making breakfast for herself. When her food was done, she sat down at the kitchen table and called her grandmother. It was wonderful to hear the older woman's voice when she answered.

"Hi, Nonna," she said. "How is Florida?"

"It's wonderful," her grandmother said. "I love it here. How is everything in Maine? How are you settling in?"

"It's been a crazy couple of days," Ellie admitted. She told her grandmother about the murder, and about the woman that she had seen. "I don't know if I'm going crazy or what, I know she's the woman I saw on the patio."

"Now, you know I'm not usually superstitious, but it definitely sounds like those woods are haunted. I'm sorry you're there alone. It must have been so frightening to see her on the patio."

"It was, but not as frightening as it was to realize that she had already been dead for forty-eight hours first. I don't know what to do. I don't think I'm crazy, but at the same time, I know what I saw, and what I saw is impossible."

"What can you do to keep ghosts away? Isn't salt supposed to do it? My own grandmother believed in those sorts of things, and every year around Halloween time she would sprinkle salt at the entrances of the house to keep the evil spirits out. I always thought she was a little bit crazy, but it might be worth a try."

"Maybe…" Ellie wasn't sure that she wanted to go that far just yet. Surely there was a rational explanation somewhere. "Anyway, it's been good talking to you. I'm glad you're enjoying Florida. I miss you, but it's good to know you're having a good time."

"I really am," her grandmother said. "Oh, I haven't told you yet, but the condo association wants to use my photo in one of their pamphlets. I'll send you one when they get printed. I'm going to be on the front page."

"I can't wait to see it," Ellie said. "I'll show everyone up here in Kittiport."

After talking for another few minutes, they said their goodbyes and Ellie hung up. Just hearing her grandmother's voice had made her feel better. She glanced to the saltshaker as she began eating her breakfast, then shook her head. No, she wouldn't resort to superstitions… not yet, anyway.

She got into work early enough to begin making their special of the week, which would be premiering the day before Halloween. She wanted to make a test pizza first. That way, she would have time to tweak the recipe if needed before serving it to her customers.

She started by preheating the oven, giving it ample time to heat up as she prepared the ingredients. She cut the butternut squash and eggplant into cubes before peeling the skin off of the fresh garlic cloves. After tossing all of the of the ingredients into a glass bowl, she drizzled olive oil and sprinkled in some dried rosemary, then tossed the vegetables until they were well-coated.

Then she spread the vegetables onto a pan and put it into the oven to roast them. While she waited, she cleaned up the mess that she had made. Just before the vegetables were ready to come out, she took one of the balls of the classic Papa Pacelli's thin crust dough out of the refrigerator and rolled it into the correct shape. She put the pizza pan into the oven so the crust could begin to pre-bake.

A few minutes later, she took both the vegetables and the pizza crust out of the oven and spread marinara sauce over the crest before placing the vegetables on top. She added crumbs of feta cheese over the toppings, then put the entire dish back into the oven.

Once the pizza was done cooking, it was difficult for her to wait for it to cool before eating it. It looked and smelled amazing, and reminded her why she enjoyed cooking so much. It was fun to be creative in the kitchen.

She wasn't disappointed when she finally tasted it. The butternut squash added just a bit of sweetness, which the sharp taste of the feta cheese complemented nicely. It was a time-consuming pizza to make, but the special would only run for a week, and she was certain that her customers would enjoy it.

By then, it was time to open the restaurant for the day. She put the rest of the pizza in the fridge for herself and her employees to snack on, then headed out to the front to unlock the doors. She was ready to start working.

It was a Friday, and one of the busier days at the pizzeria, so both Jacob and Rose were working with her that evening. Jacob had been spending more time at the restaurant then doing deliveries lately, but since they didn't have a dedicated delivery driver currently, he and Rose were back to taking turns delivering the pizzas. Ever since Sabrina's death, she had been anxious whenever one of her employees went on a delivery. She wished that there was something she could do to help ensure their safety, but other than warning them to keep a close eye on their surroundings, she was almost helpless. About half of the pizzeria's business came from deliveries. She couldn't very well stop them completely, though she would never ask employees to make a delivery if they didn't feel safe.

With Halloween only a few days away, her customers were in high spirits. Both children and adults seem to love the holiday. She was looking forward to next Tuesday, when she would get to dress up and hand out candy at work.

She was pleasantly surprised later in the day by a visit from Joanna and her husband. She took a short break to sit with them while their order was cooking.

"So, about the small business club, I have a friend in Benton Harbor that owns a bakery. Would it be okay if I asked her to come, or is only for people who live in Kittiport?"

"Go ahead and tell her about it," Ellie said. "I'm happy for anyone who lives nearby to come. Benton Harbor is pretty close by, and I think it would be nice to get to know people from there too."

"Okay, I'm sure she will be glad to hear about it. Just let me know when you have thought more about it. I might know a couple of other people that would be interested as well."

"I will," Ellie said.

"How is your wedding planning coming along?" her friend asked. "I didn't get a chance to ask you before."

"It's going well," she said. "I already spoke to Dan at the community center about using it as a venue for the wedding, and he gave me a couple of dates that might work."

"Dan Asado?" Steve asked. "I know him. We went to college together. It's been nice to catch up with him."

"It's a small world," Ellie said, smiling. "You'll get used to it soon enough living in this town. Everyone knows everyone else."

"You are engaged to the local sheriff, aren't you?" Steve asked. She nodded. "Do you know if he ever confirmed the identity of the dead woman they found? I know it's only been a day, but I want to know if it's Melanie. If it is, I feel terrible for her family. She was close with her sister and her mother, and they will be devastated."

"I don't know, but I can check for you," she said. She frowned, remembering that Steve was possibly a suspect in the case. If it *was* Melanie, Russell would probably bring him in for questioning. She didn't know if she should even be talking to him, but she didn't know how she could remove herself from the conversation without seeming rude.

"Oh, I really hope it wasn't her," Joanna said. "I only met her once, but she seemed nice. Maybe that's a weird thing to say about my husband's ex-girlfriend, but they dated before I even met him. I can't hold that against her."

"I hope it's not her, too," Ellie said. She really did. She liked Joanna a lot, but if Russell ended up arresting her husband, she didn't know if their friendship could survive that. She hoped for all of their sakes that the murder victim wasn't Steve's ex.

After a couple of minutes, Rose signaled that their food was ready and Ellie rose with relief to bring it out. She would call Russell as soon as possible to figure out if he had confirmed the identity of the murder victim yet. If they hadn't, then that would be good news for Steve and Joanna, but bad news for the victim's family. Finding out her identity would be the first step to figuring out who had killed her.

CHAPTER NINE

The next day was Saturday, which Ellie had completely off from work. She enjoyed the opportunity to sleep in, glad that she didn't have anything scheduled for that day. The house was oddly silent without her grandmother moving around downstairs, at least until Marlowe began to call for attention.

Ellie sat up in bed, yawning, while Bunny stretched on the pillow beside her. The sun was shining through her sheer curtains, and she felt pleasantly well rested. It was a good start to what she hoped would be a relaxing weekend.

After going downstairs to care for the animals, she took a cup of coffee to the back patio while Bunny explored the yard. It wasn't until she heard her phone ring inside that she forced herself to get up and really start her day.

The call was from Russell, who had news that she wasn't happy to hear. "We finally got the call back," he said. "The deceased woman is Melanie. Liam is heading out to bring Steve in for questioning right now."

Ellie sighed. It was bad news. It would be even worse if Steve had really been the one to kill her. Did Joanna know? She couldn't imagine her friend being okay with a murder, but there was no telling what someone would do for their spouse.

"Thank you for letting me know," she said. "I really hope it's not him."

"Me too," her fiancé said. "Could you do me a favor and not mention this to Joanna or Shannon? I trust Shannon, but I don't want to put her in a position where she might have to lie to one of her friends."

"Of course. Will you call me when you know more?"

"I will," he promised. "I should get going now. I just wanted to let you know."

She said goodbye and hung up, feeling conflicted. If the killer wasn't Steve, then that meant that they would have no leads. At least now that they knew for sure who the dead woman was, they could begin exploring who else might have had a possible motive.

She spent most of the morning cooking and cleaning, even pulling Marlowe's cage outside – without the bird in it – to spray it down before it got too cold out. A little bit after noon, when she had eaten a pleasant lunch alone outside, she got another call, this time from Shannon. She answered, expecting her friend to want to talk about Steve's trip to the sheriff's department. She was surprised when Shannon didn't seem to know about it at all. While she had promised Russell not to tell her friend about it, Shannon usually had a pretty good grasp on the town's grapevine of gossip. It was rare for Ellie to know something that she didn't.

"Do you want to get together this evening?" her friend asked. "James is going to be out of town, so I thought I could come over and we could spend some time together. We haven't really had much of a chance to talk since you got back."

"Sure," Ellie said. "That sounds nice. What time do you think you'll be here?"

"Would around three work? I'll bring some stuff for us to make for dinner, as well as a couple of movies, if you want. We'll just have a nice girl's night in."

"I would love that," Ellie said. "I'll see you then."

Shannon arrived shortly after three, loaded down with grocery bags and DVDs. Ellie let her inside and help her carry everything into the kitchen. While her friend gave Bunny a couple of dog treats, Ellie began unpacking the bags. Her friend had brought the ingredients to make a cake, some sort of chicken dish, and alcohol-free margaritas. Ellie smiled. Being pregnant had given her friend some limitations, but she always seemed to find ways to get around them. She was glad that she was able to be a part of Shannon's journey. It was odd to think that her friend would soon be a mother.

Ellie took the liberty of cutting up all of the ingredients needed for the creamy chicken casserole while her friend read through the directions and pulled out the spices, sauces, and seasonings that they would need.

Once the main dish was in the oven, they prepared the cake mix. They filled the two round pans with the batter, then placed them in the oven underneath the casserole dish. The hard part done, they cleaned the kitchen together, then retreated to the living room to start their movie.

It was one of the most pleasant afternoons Ellie had had for a long time. It was nice to simply sit with her friend and talk about inconsequential matters. They avoided the topic of the murder, for which Ellie was grateful. She had spent enough time thinking about it over the past few days. Until Russell called her back to tell her whether or not he thought Steve was guilty, there wasn't any point in dwelling on the matter.

When the food was done, they took the cakes out and left them on the counter to cool while they dug into the casserole. Bunny waited under the table, begging. Ellie smiled at the little dog, but otherwise ignored her. Her grandmother had been the one to begin the bad habit of feeding her table scraps. Now that the older woman was living in Florida, Ellie thought that it was time to break the habit.

"Did you have any problems with her while you were watching her?" she asked her friend.

"None," Shannon said. "She was an angel. If I wasn't going to have a baby soon, I might even think about getting a dog myself. I don't really want to deal with an infant and the dog at the same time, though."

"That's understandable," Ellie said. "You'll have your hands full enough as it is."

"And so will you, with a new husband," Shannon said, grinning at her. "How are the wedding plans coming along?"

"Well, I bought a beautiful dress while I was in Florida," she said. "It should be here in a couple of weeks."

"I can't wait to see it," her friend said. "Do you have the date set yet?"

"No, not yet," Ellie said. "We have a couple of dates picked out, but Russell has to talk to his parents. He's supposed to be calling them this weekend to see what day would work best for them. Which reminds me, I've got to call my mom too."

"You still haven't told her, have you?"

"No. I know I should. I should have told her when I first got engaged. The longer I put it off, the harder it gets."

"I'm sure she'll be fine about it," her friend said. "Even if she's not, who cares? It's not her wedding, it's yours. You're an adult. You lead your own life. It's no one's business but yours when you get engaged."

"Thanks. I'll feel a lot better once I've told her, I know, I just have to get around to actually doing it."

"Do you want to do it while I'm here?"

Ellie wrinkled her nose. While she might appreciate the moral support from her friend, she had too much on her mind to even think about calling her mother right now.

"I think I'll wait until after things get figured out about the murder," she said.

"Okay. Just let me know if you want me around when you call her. From what I remember, she can be rather… overbearing."

Overbearing was one way to describe her mom. Ellie smiled. She couldn't wait until her own mother met Russell's mother. Those two women would give each other a run for their money.

They spent the rest of the evening watching movies together and snacking on the cake. By the time Shannon was preparing to go home, it was late, and dark outside.

"I'll help you wash our plates before I leave," her friend said. "I would feel bad leaving you with all of these dishes to do in the morning."

While they were washing the dishes together, Bunny started barking in the other room. Ellie sighed and set the plate down. She was probably barking at Marlowe again; the bird had begun teasing her with food, enjoying the reaction she got from the dog.

She walked into the hall and was surprised to find that Bunny wasn't by the bird's cage. She was barking from the living room. Ellie walked in there and felt a shiver of apprehension when she saw the dog staring at the window.

Cautiously, she walked towards the dark pane of glass and peered outside. At first, she didn't see anything, but as her eyes adjusted to the lack of light, she some movement at the edge of her yard. She thought she saw a flash of white, and head of dark hair. Her blood turned cold.

Scooping the little dog up, she turned and ran from the living room. She burst into the kitchen.

"Shannon, hurry. That woman in white is back. She's in the yard."

Her friend dropped the dish she was washing into the sink and hurried to join her. By the time they made it to the window in the living room, the woman was nowhere to be seen. Ellie put Bunny down. The little dog sniffed at the floor, then looked up at her, her tail wagging and the incident already forgotten.

CHAPTER TEN

For the next few days, Ellie hardly ate or slept. Seeing the woman in white once, she could have shrugged off as an odd occurrence that would never happen again. The second time, she hadn't been completely sure that she had even seen the same person. She couldn't ignore it the third time it happened.

Steve had been released later the same day that Liam had taken him in for questioning. With no physical evidence of his presence at the crime scene, and his continued denial that he had even known that Melanie was in town, they hadn't been able to hold him.

Every time Ellie heard a noise, she thought that it was either the ghostly woman or her killer coming back to the house. She was jumpier than ever, and was relieved when it was time to go back to work on Monday.

By the time Tuesday came around, she was exhausted. She had wanted to enjoy Halloween, but instead, all she could think about was how nice it would be when the day was over. She was sick of being so frightened at her own home. All she wanted was a good night's sleep. If she could just have one night's sleep, she could go back to being frightened in the morning. The last thing that she wanted was to stay up late wearing an uncomfortable costume and handing out candy while trying to stay awake.

Still, when she pulled on her costume that morning, she forced herself to smile. Halloween was a fun day for the kids, and she didn't want to wreck it by being in a bad mood. She had a huge bag of mixed candy ready to go. She was dressed as an elf, complete with glued on pointy ears. It was a fun costume, but it wasn't exactly the warmest thing. Dan had been right; it was one of the coldest days yet. No wonder some of the children wanted to go trick-or-treating at the community center instead of wandering the freezing streets.

When she got to the pizzeria, she pulled out the nicest glass bowls they had and dumped the candy into them. For the earlier part of the day, she would simply leave them on the counter and allow customers to take a piece or two as they made their orders. When it got later in the evening and the trick-or-treaters began to arrive, she or one of her employees would sit outside with the bowl.

A few minutes before opening, Pete arrived in a knight's outfit, complete with real chain mail. "Impressive," she said. "If the murderer shows up here tonight, you'll be safe."

"It's heavy," he admitted. "I may end up taking it off later. Still, it will be fun to wear for a while."

After that, they were too busy to talk much. It was the second day that Ellie was running the autumn harvest pizza special of the week, and preparing the toppings kept her running around the kitchen. She could only make so much of the squash, eggplant, and garlic at once. The pizza was popular, which was a good thing, but also meant that they were going through a lot of the ingredients.

After a couple hours, she switched places with Pete, who took off his chain mail and worked in the kitchen while she manned the front. It was still early enough that most people weren't in costume, but a few were, especially children who had come from school events. She enjoyed seeing the princesses, pirates, dragons, and zombies who wandered into her shop. Thinking of Shannon and the child that she would have next year, she smiled. She thought her friend would enjoy this.

Gradually, it began to get darker, and soon enough she saw trick-or-treaters walking the streets outside. Many of the local businesses had opted to participate in the trick-or-treating, so she wasn't the only one sitting outside on a chair with a bowl of candy in her lap. As she sat there, she thought more about the small business club that she was planning to start. She was glad that Joanna knew a couple of people that might join, because she didn't. Sure, she knew which businesses around town were owned by which people, but she didn't know their owners personally. That was part of the reason why she was starting the club, but it might make it difficult to get members in the first place.

Even though it was chilly out, it was a pleasant evening, handing out candy and talking to the townspeople. Her mood was dampened when Joanna and Steve walked past her. The other woman looked at her, frowned, then quickly strode by on the sidewalk without stopping. Ellie bit her lip, watching her and her husband go into a bar a few doors down. It wasn't her fault that Steve had been taken in for questioning. Joanna probably thought that Ellie had been spying on them when they stopped to get lunch together. She just wished that she could explain the truth to the other woman.

She did have a reason to brighten up when Dan walked by and made a beeline for her. "I thought I recognized you," he said. "I'm just on my way to meet a friend for a drink, but since you're right here, we might as well talk. There's no rush, of course. Do you know what date you're going to choose yet? The sooner I can get it locked down for you, the better. I wouldn't want to disappoint the sheriff and his fiancée on their wedding day."

Chuckling, she said, "Yes, we have a date. Can you reserve the twenty-fourth of February for us?

83

"I'll mark it down," he said. "Once again, congratulations."

She smiled as she watched him walk away. Her wedding date was locked down, and she had a dress. She was doing pretty well.

Trick-or-treating lasted for a couple of hours. As it got later, darker, and colder out, the average age of the people in costumes seemed to rise. Eventually, she just dropped the rest of the candy into a teenager's bucket and went inside, relishing the cocoon of warm air that surrounded her inside the pizzeria.

It was almost time to start closing for the evening. She fought back a yawn and found herself wishing that she hadn't offered to go with Russell while he patrolled the town. Normally she would have enjoyed it, but tonight she was so tired from her lack of sleep that she wasn't looking forward to it much at all.

"I need coffee," she muttered. The pizzeria had an old, temperamental coffee machine that she and her employees used to keep themselves awake. She started the process of making a cup of coffee for herself while she and Pete began cleaning up.

With the bitter drink in a thermos to keep her awake, she pulled her jacket on over her elf costume and left out the back door, locking it behind her. She waved goodbye to her employee and waited in the parking lot for a few minutes until she saw the headlights of Russell's truck pull up. She climbed into the passenger seat, hoping that it would be a quiet night. Maybe she could doze during the ride.

"How was your evening?" he asked her as she got settled.

"It wasn't terrible," she said. She told her about running into Dan and settling the date for the wedding, but also mentioned Joanna and the look that the other woman had given her.

"I'm sorry," he said. "I know she's your friend, and I wouldn't have taken Steve in unless I thought there was a chance that he had done it."

"So now you're certain that he didn't?" she asked.

"Not certain, no, we just didn't find anything at all that might incriminate him. While he didn't have an alibi, he swore up and down he hadn't contacted her in years. He even offered us his phone as evidence. We found no physical evidence to connect him to the crime scene. We still haven't been able to find the weapon. Even though I still think he's the most likely person to have committed the crime, we had to let him go."

"I'm sorry," Ellie said. "It must be frustrating, to think that he did it but not be able to find anything on him. If he is guilty, then I hope

85

you find what you need soon. Whoever killed that poor woman deserves to go to prison, whether or not he's married to a friend of mine."

"We're working as hard as we can," he said. "But tonight, we are taking a break in the case to patrol the town. Wearing a costume seems to make people feel free to do whatever they want, and it's our job to make sure no one gets hurt."

CHAPTER ELEVEN

Either the coffee was beginning to work, or riding around with Russell was turning out to be a lot more interesting than she had thought. Normally when she rode with him, things were pretty quiet. They would sit for long stretches of time on the busiest roads in and out of town waiting for people who were speeding around dangerous corners, and occasionally respond to calls. Ellie had watched as Russell unlocked a car door in the heat of the summer for a lady who had accidentally locked her dog inside, and take information on the missing bike for a couple of kids who swore that theirs had been stolen.

Halloween night was different. They drove slowly through the streets, with Russell's attention on the dark sidewalk and empty yards. The radio in the vehicle was on, and it was filled with chatter between Mrs. Lafferre, Liam, and Bethany. Mrs. Lafferre was acting as a dispatcher, and kept reporting to them as the calls came in.

"Mrs. Hammontree on Barry Street says that kids are driving by and throwing eggs at her house. This has happened a couple of times tonight. She's a teacher at the local high school."

"I'll get out there," Liam said. "I'm only a couple of streets away. Tell her an officer will come and park across the street from her house. Next time those kids come by, I'll pull them over and give him a good talking to."

Russell smiled, turning the radio down. "I'd love to see those kids faces when Liam turns on his flashing lights," he said. "He'll give them a good scare, and hopefully they'll all go home for the rest of the night."

"I feel bad for their teacher," Ellie said. "That's not a great way to repay someone teaching you."

"Stuff like this happens every year at Halloween," her fiancé said. "Most of it is little pranks, mostly harmless, but still illegal since they have to do with destruction of property, or trespassing. Every once in a while, we'll get something bigger. A couple of years ago, someone tried to start a bonfire in their yard. They lived in one of the more crowded subdivisions in town, and decided that burning old furniture in a huge pile with a bunch of gasoline was the way to go. That one ended in an arrest, but the man responsible only spent the night in jail before going home, sober, the next day. He didn't actually manage to get the fire lit, thankfully."

"It sounds so much more interesting than your usual nights," she said.

"I prefer a quiet night," he said. "When everything's calm, it means no one is getting in trouble. I never like arresting people. These are all my neighbors and my friends. I know they're good people at heart, but sometimes things can get a little crazy. Speaking of…"

He turned the dial on the radio and Ellie listened to Mrs. Lafferre say, "We've got a couple of suspicious people called in by one Ms. Carry Lightwood. She said they're standing in front of her neighbor's house, where no one is home, and arguing."

Ellie frowned, giving Russell a worried look. "That's my neighbor," she said. "Do you think she's talking about my house?"

"Can we have the address?" Russell asked the radio. Mrs. Lafferre responded. Ellie and Russell exchanged a look. It was her address. "We're on our way," he replied.

Ellie sat up, gripping the edges of her seat anxiously as Russell turned on his lights and sped through town. Who could possibly be at her house? What did they want? Her exhaustion seemed to have disappeared, to be replaced by worry.

After what seemed like an eternity, they neared her house. Russell slowed down, but kept his lights flashing as he pulled into her driveway behind the vehicle that was parked there. There were two people on the front porch, and they both turned to look at them as she and Russell got out of the car.

In the dark, it took Ellie a moment to recognize the people; Joanna and Steve. She breathed a sigh of relief. Her greatest fear was that there had been a break in and the animals might have been hurt.

"What are the two of you doing here?" she asked, annoyed, as she approached the porch.

"I'm sorry," Joanna said. "We met a friend at the bar and Steve was drinking, and we were talking about you, and he wanted to come here to ask why everyone thinks he killed Melanie. I told him it would be better to just talk to you in the morning, but he insisted and I thought that it would make him feel better if he heard it from you that questioning him was just a formality."

"My car isn't even here," Ellie said. "You could tell I wasn't home."

"We thought it might be parked in the garage," Joanna said. "Anyway, I'm sorry. We were just about to leave. I never in a million years meant for the police to be called."

Ellie sighed. Russell was standing behind her, a comforting and supportive presence. Steve was obviously drunk, and Joanna looked upset.

"It's fine," Ellie said. "We can talk tomorrow. Why don't the two of you just go home now?"

"We will," Joanna said, shooting an anxious look at Russell. "And Ellie, I'm sorry if I was acting rude to you earlier today when I didn't stop and say anything. I admit, I was pretty mad when Steve got taken in for questioning. I thought that if you are a real friend, you would've told us. I guess I've come to realize that you really couldn't have told us anything. I'm sure anything the sheriff tells you, you promise to keep confidential. And I guess if you had told us beforehand that Steve was a suspect, it just would have made things worse. We would've both been worried for days before he got taken in for questioning."

"I'm sorry I couldn't say anything," Ellie said. "I hope this doesn't wreck our friendship."

"Not at all," Joanna said. "Thanks for forgiving me, Ellie. I'll see you later. Have a good evening."

Russell got back into his truck to back it out of the driveway so Joanna and Steve could leave. Joanna was wearing a large, fluffy coat, which she took off as she got behind the driver's wheel. When her friend leaned forward to turn on the overhead light and search the vehicle for something, Ellie noticed long, ragged scratches on her friend's arms. The light clicked off, and the vehicle started. Before she could say anything, the car pulled out of the driveway and turned towards town.

She hurried up to Russell's window as he pulled the truck back into the driveway. "Did you see that?" she asked.

"See what?"

"Joanna's arms were all scratched up." She bit her lip, trying to believe that what she was about to say was wrong. "Think about it. She has scratches on her arms, like someone might get from pushing their way through the undergrowth. The victim is her husband's ex. Melanie visited this town for a reason, but Steve refuses to say why. If they were having an affair and Joanna found out, wouldn't it be motive for murder?"

She saw comprehension dawn on Russell's face as he connected the dots as well. "You're right, Ellie. I can't believe we didn't see it before. Who knows why they were really here. I'm going to go see if I can catch them before they get back. I need to bring Joanna in and ask her some questions. Will you be all right here? I can pick you up when I'm done to tell you what happened and bring you back to the pizzeria to get your car."

"I'll be fine here," she promised. "Just call me before you head back. I may be in bed. Be careful, Russell. I really hope it's not her."

"So do I," her fiancé said. "But hope never solved a murder."

CHAPTER TWELVE

Ellie watched as her fiancé pulled away. She felt miserable. She liked Joanna. She didn't want to think that the woman could be responsible for a crime like this, but the pieces fit together too perfectly. The woman would have had a motive, and scratches on her arm might be physical evidence that she was in the forest at the time of Melanie's death.

She turned the key in the lock and let herself inside, shutting the door behind her. Bunny greeted her happily, and she bent down to pet the little dog. Despite her concerns, she was exhausted. Part of her wanted to stay up and wait for Russell to come back to tell her what he had found out. Another part of her wanted to collapse into her bed and wait until morning to get the whole thing settled.

She opted for a compromise. She would make a cup of green tea and drink in the kitchen, and if she didn't feel more awake afterward once the small amount of caffeine had had a chance to do its work, she would go upstairs to bed, but leave her clothes on in case she wanted to get up to visit with Russell in the middle of the night when he was done with Joanna.

The routine of making tea was a comforting one. Her grandmother had made tea hundreds of times in this kitchen, and she felt closer to the older woman as she boiled the pot of water and put a tea bag in one of the mugs. She missed her grandmother. Things just weren't the same. Especially with everything that had been happening, she didn't feel comfortable there. At least in a few months, Russell would be living there with her. By then, she wanted to have made some changes to the home so that it felt more like their shared house, as opposed to them living at her grandmother's house. Nonna had said that she was free to do whatever she wanted with the home, and even though Ellie had been reluctant to make those changes just yet, she knew that in the long run, it would be the best for her marriage if she and Russell had their own space.

With the patio light on, Ellie sat at the kitchen table and gazed outside. She couldn't see anything beyond the circle of light, and wondered not for the first time how everything linked together. If Joanna was the killer, how did that explain the woman that she kept seeing? Even though she kept telling herself that there had to be a logical explanation, some small part of her still thought that she might have seen a ghost. The thought was both chilling and sad. Oddly enough, however, the thought of the ghost was less frightening than the thought that there had been a living woman walking around the woods and haunting her. A ghost couldn't hurt her, but a flesh and blood person could.

A low growl sounded from the floor behind her. Ellie turned to see Bunny staring out the glass door, her small body tense as she gazed into the darkness. Goosebumps rose on Ellie's skin. She got up and turned off the light inside the kitchen to prevent who or what ever was outside from seeing inside, and pressed her face to the window, trying desperately to see beyond the patio light.

Whatever was out there was well beyond the edge of the darkness. She couldn't see anything. Bunny, however, was certainly sensing something. She had never seen the little dog so worked up.

Knowing that there was no way she could ignore her dog's warning, she opened the pantry and felt around on the shelves until she found the powerful flashlight that her grandmother kept there. She put her feet into the sandals that she kept by the back door for when she let Bunny outside, then turned the patio light on and slipped through the door, making sure the dog stayed inside. The last thing she needed was to have the little dog chase after something in the pitch-black woods.

With the patio and kitchen lights both off, she felt both blind and invisible. She was silent and unmoving for a moment, listening to the sounds around her and trying to identify what Bunny might have heard. After a couple of seconds, she heard the loud crack of a branch breaking somewhere in the woods in front of her.

She did her best to aim in the dark, then click on the flashlight. The beam illuminated the edge of the forest. Ellie swept it across the trees, then froze when she caught a flash of white. It was the woman. The ghost? No, a ghost wouldn't break branches while it was walking through the forest. This was a living person.

Whoever it was seemed to realize that they had been seen, and they froze. Ellie kept the beam of light trained on them. The person was hidden mostly behind a tree, with only their white clothing visible. She didn't know which one of them would move first. She hadn't brought her phone outside with her. Things had just happened too quickly.

From behind her, Bunny let out a sharp bark. That seemed to do it. The person in the woods moved, crashing through the trees. Ellie hesitated for a moment, then figured if the person was running away from her, they probably weren't too dangerous. She remembered the dark stains on the person's clothing when the woman had approached her patio door the week before. What if this person was hurt, and had been wandering around the woods since the attack looking for help? If the person had a head injury or was mentally ill, it could explain why they were so wary and hadn't approached anyone. It was cold out, and Ellie couldn't let a frightened, possibly injured person vanish into the woods. Every time she had seen the person, they had done their best to avoid her. She wondered, as she ran to the yard, why she had been so afraid before. Whoever this woman was, she was the one that was frightened.

"Hello?" she called as she entered the woods. "I want to help!"

There was no answer. She heard movement ahead of her, and kept moving forward. She was grateful that she had remembered to put on her sandals, even though they didn't do much to protect her feet from the cold. The forest floor was littered with twigs and sharp rocks, and she wouldn't want to try to walk through it in the dark, barefoot.

"If there's someone out here, I want to help you," she said. "I've seen you hanging around out there. If you're hurt, I can call an ambulance."

There was no response, but whoever was moving in the forest ahead of her stopped. Ellie bit her lip, feeling another flutter of fear in her chest. Maybe she was being foolish to do this, but part of her wanted to keep pushing forward. Russell was out there right now, confronting a possible murder. Should she just hide in her house when there was an injured person outside that needed help? She wanted to be brave, like him, and not let fear control her.

There was a sudden noise behind her, making Ellie jump. She spun around, the light of the flashlight cutting through the trees. The beam illuminated a man's face, looming only feet away from her.

CHAPTER THIRTEEN

Ellie let out a sharp scream and jumped backward, almost tripping over a branch.

"Dan?" she asked, incredulous.

"Ellie?" he said, sounding just as surprised as she was. "What are you doing out here?"

"I live right there," she said, gesturing back towards her house. "What are *you* doing here?"

"I'm just looking for…" He frowned, looking from her flashlight to her sandaled feet. "Did you lose something?"

"No," she replied shortly. She had a sudden, dark suspicion. Dan and Steve had known each other for years. That meant that it was possible that Dan had known Melanie as well. What his motive to kill the other woman might have been, she couldn't know, but the simple fact that he was out here, less than a quarter of a mile away from where the woman had been killed, was enough to make her fear the worst.

"I think you should go back inside," he said.

She nodded, clenching her teeth together. Yes, she would go inside. She would go inside, and call Russell immediately. She was just about to edge around him when she saw him tense. It wasn't much more than a twitch, but his hand had definitely moved towards his pocket, which she could see looked lumpy and heavy, as if something was inside it.

Something metal, like a gun? Her mind raced. He knew that she was engaged to the sheriff. It would be reasonable for him to assume that she would mention to Russell that she had seen him out here in the woods. If he had killed Melanie, that would be a link to the crime scene that he wouldn't be able to afford. On the other hand, if no one knew that he was out here tonight other than her, then he might be able to get away with shooting her without anyone being the wiser about who had done it. A dead woman couldn't talk.

Ellie froze, no longer wanting to turn her back to him. His frown deepened. "This really isn't the place for a woman wearing an elf costume and sandals," he said.

She had forgotten about the costume. She must look ridiculous out here, but that was the least of her worries. What could she do? If he had a gun, then her heavy flashlight wouldn't be much use against him. There was no way she could defend herself if he decided to shoot her, but he seemed reluctant to do anything to her face.

"You never answered me," she said, trying to keep her voice casual. "What are you looking for out here? Maybe I can help you. I know these woods pretty well."

That was a lie, of course. She hardly knew the trails in the state park, and certainly couldn't navigate her way out here where there were no trails at all.

"Just something I lost," he said vaguely. "I wouldn't want to keep you. You go on back inside and get warmed up."

"I think I'll stay," she said. "I wouldn't feel right leaving you out here alone." She kept her voice as friendly as possible.

He frowned, and she saw his fingers twitch towards his pocket again.

"Russell should be back soon," she added, hoping the mention of her fiancé might make him back down. "Maybe he could come out and help us look."

When she saw the look on his face, she realized that she had made a mistake in mentioning the sheriff. He reached his hand into his pocket, and sure enough withdrew a pistol. Aiming at her, he said, "I really didn't want to have to do this. I'm sorry, Ellie. I have to put myself first."

She heard the safety click off. She closed her eyes, not wanting to see him fire the shot that would kill her. The shot never came. Instead, someone let out a strangled shout, and there was a crashing sound as branches broke. Ellie open her eyes just in time to see a woman wearing a long white coat rush toward Dan. Dan didn't have time to readjust his aim before she slammed into him. Ellie saw a flash of metal as the woman buried a knife in Dan's abdomen. He dropped the gun and stumbled backwards, staring in shock at the handle of the blade that was sticking out of him.

"That's my knife," he said, his eyes wide with shock. Suddenly, the pain seemed to hit him and he sank to his knees.

The woman was staring at him, her face contorted with fury. "You killed my sister," she said. "I saw the whole thing. Now just tell me, where is the tape?"

With his fingers shaking, Dan managed to reach into his other pocket and remove an old cassette tape. He put it on the ground.

"Please don't kill me," he panted. "Call an ambulance. I don't want to die."

The woman bent down and picked up the tape. Ellie saw that she was wearing a long white trench coat, which in her panic the other night, she must have confused for a dress.

"You're the one I've been seeing, aren't you?" she asked. The woman turned to face her, her fury fizzling out into something more manageable.

"I recognize, you, you live in that house back there. My name is Valerie. I'm Melanie's older sister. I'm sorry if I frightened you. I was going to ask you if you had heard anything the night before, but I thought better of it, so I left."

"I thought you were a ghost," Ellie said. "You look so much like your sister, and you were both wearing white."

"I didn't even think of that connection," the woman said. "I was only wearing this coat because it's the only warm thing I brought. It was supposed to be part of a Halloween costume, but then I got it muddy in the woods that first night, so I just kept wearing it."

Dan groaned, and both women looked down at him. "I don't have my phone on me," Ellie said, realizing that they needed to get the man help. It was one thing for Valerie to attack him when he was about to shoot her, but they couldn't very well let him bleed to death like this.

"I have my cell phone," the other woman said. "Will you wait here while the police arrive? I don't want to be alone with him."

Ellie nodded. She waited while Valerie called 911, then asked her a question that she had been wondering. "How did you find his knife? Is it the same one that he used to kill your sister?"

"Yes," Valerie said. "It's a long story, I suppose I'll tell it to you if we have time."

"Go ahead," Ellie said. "I'll wait here with you until the paramedics get here. We might as well talk."

"Well, all of this started years ago when my sister lived in Portland. She started dating Dan after she broke up with a guy that he was friends with, Steve. The thing is, she didn't realize that Dan was already married at that point. When she found out, she took a video of them in a… compromising situation… then threatened to tell his wife if he didn't give her money to pay off her debts. She told me all of this a couple of years after it happened."

"So, he killed her over something that happened years ago?" Ellie said. "That's horrible."

"Not exactly," Valerie said. She sighed. "This part is somewhat my fault. Melanie has always really been bad with money. She opens as many credit cards as she can, and maxes them all out. She had sunk into debt again pretty badly over this past year. She still had the old tape of them together, and figured that she could do the same thing she had done before. Her plan was to come up here and ask Dan for money, or she would tell his wife what they had done all those years ago."

"So, she was blackmailing him?"

Valerie closed her eyes. "Yes. She convinced me to come with her, I only agreed to keep her safe. We met him in these woods on our way to a Halloween party. She met him by herself, with me hanging back to support her if she needed it. I didn't agree with what she was doing, but she was my sister. I didn't want her to get hurt. As it turned out, I wasn't much help anyway. It all happened so quickly. She was about to hand the tape over when I saw this man stab her. I shouted out and he fled, leaving Melanie to struggle through the forest. He dropped the knife and I picked it up, thinking that I could turn it in to the police so they could use it as evidence against him. By the time I reached Melanie, she had collapsed and I couldn't find a pulse. I tried to stop the bleeding, but I had to give up. Her heart had stopped and she wasn't breathing anymore. I looked all over for the tape, knowing that it would be the thing to put Dan in jail. I was so sure she had dropped it somewhere, and I came out every day to look for it. I didn't think that she had actually handed it off to him, but she must have."

"Why didn't you go to the police?" Ellie asked.

"I was selfish," Valerie admitted. "The more I thought about it, the more I realized that what we were doing was illegal. Blackmail is a crime. She was already dead, but I wasn't. I didn't want to go to jail for something like that. I figured if I found the tape, I could mail it and the knife to the police anonymously. That way I wouldn't get in trouble for being involved in this, but she would still get the justice she deserved. I held onto the knife, and kept looking. I went into town today just to get freshened up at the community center, and that's when Dan saw me. I didn't say anything to him, but I knew he recognized me. He must've followed me out here, and when he saw me going to the woods, he would have put two and two together and figured out that I knew what had happened to my sister. I'm sure he was coming out here to silence me, so thanks for following me. You probably saved my life."

"You probably saved mine," Ellie said.

They both looked at Dan, who was still whimpering, his fingers around the knife. He knew enough not to pull it out, and Ellie thought that he would probably hold on until the paramedics arrived. She would stay with Valerie until they got there. The other woman might not have made the best choices, but unlike Dan, she seemed to be a good person at heart, and Ellie couldn't leave her alone after all of this.

EPILOGUE

Ellie sat in the waiting room at the sheriff's department, reading some of the old magazines that Mrs. Lafferre had stacked on the table. For once, she wasn't here to see Russell. When the door to the back opened, she looked up to see Valerie coming towards her. Now that she no longer had on her white coat, Ellie could easily see differences between her and her sister. They had the same long, dark hair, but the similarities ended there.

"Thank you so much," Valerie said. "You didn't have to do this."

"I wanted to," Ellie said. "Just don't make me regret it, okay? Show up for your court date."

"I will," she said. "I want to give my sister a chance for justice, and I can't do that if I'm on the run."

Valerie had been arrested on obstruction of justice charges. Ellie had decided to post bail for her, wanting the woman to be able to join her family for her sister's funeral service. She thought that it was a safe bet. She didn't think that Valerie would run. She hoped that when her court date came, the judge would go easy on her. Yes, she should have gone to the police immediately, but at the same time, she had just witnessed her sister's violent death. She probably hadn't been thinking clearly.

"I'll give you a ride to the motel you were staying at," she said. "What happened to your jacket?"

"Oh, that? I threw it away. It was all muddy and torn. Halloween's over, anyway."

"I'm not sure what you were supposed to be, but you made a great ghost," Ellie said, giving her a small smile as she rose.

"I'm so sorry about scaring you," the woman said. "I wasn't thinking straight then. Looking back on it, I can see how that might have freaked you out just a little bit."

"It certainly made life interesting for a few days," Ellie said. "And Valerie, I'm sorry about your sister. I know you two were close. I can't imagine losing someone like that."

"Sometimes it still doesn't feel real," Valerie said. "We were close in age, and we were really more like friends than sisters. I don't know what my life is going to be like without her. She was always there for me when I needed her. She may have had her problems, but I loved her. I'm going to miss her. I hope Dan rots in prison for the rest of his life."

"Russell will do everything he can to see that Dan gets the maximum sentence," Ellie said.

The two of them got into Ellie's car. The town seemed deflated somehow after the holiday. The decorations were slowly being taken down, and the trees seemed to have lost even more leaves overnight. It was beginning to look more like winter than autumn.

It was a somber day, with dark clouds above them threatening rain and the wind gusting occasionally, causing dry leaves to fly across the road. Ellie and Valerie drove to the motel in silence. Ellie was still shaken by everything that happened that night in the woods. She had come close to dying. If Valerie had been a second later, or had been a little less brave, it would be her funeral that Russell was getting ready for.

Even though Valerie had made some poor choices, her heart went out to the other woman. Posting bail for her was the least she could do. Valerie had saved her life, and that wasn't something that she took lightly. Thanks to the woman in the seat next to her, Ellie still had her future. She would have years to appreciate all of the hard work she had put into the pizzerias. She would be able to go through with her wedding with Russell, and get married to the man that she loved. Thanks to Valerie, she'd be able to see her grandmother come home next year, and see her best friend's baby be born. She felt a warmth rise inside of her, a simple love for life. She was grateful that she had been given another chance, and she didn't want to waste it.

11340129R00063